The Southwest Adventures of Tommy and Maggie

Written and Illustrated by

Marilyn L. Alexander

To: Sandra
Dreams do Come true...
God Bless...

AuthorHouse™
1663 Liberty Drive
Bloomington, IN 47403
www.authorhouse.com
Phone: 1-800-839-8640

First published by AuthorHouse 11/24/2009

ISBN: 978-1-4389-8251-9 (sc)

Printed in the United States of America
Bloomington, Indiana

This book is printed on acid-free paper.

For:

Dot Leininger and Sarah Rivers, my beloved grandmothers, I know you are both smiling down from heaven, my first book is dedicated to you both.

Maggie is a black dog.

Tommy is a yellow dog.

They are "best friends".

They live in the desert outside
Albuquerque, New Mexico.

They like to spend the day running and
playing in the desert.

The desert is a fun place. There are so many interesting things for Tommy and Maggie to do.

They like to chase the desert animals. They like to chase the Jack Rabbits that have long ears and jump really high.

They like to chase the Roadrunners that run really fast.

They like to roll around and chase each
other in the desert sand.

One day while playing in the desert they spotted a coyote on top of a hill beside them.

The coyote spotted them.

The coyote starting running toward
Tommy and Maggie as fast as he could.

Maggie and Tommy looked at each other.

Maggie was afraid.

Tommy was also afraid.

The coyote came closer and closer.

Maggie and Tommy started running as fast as they could run.

They ran...

And ran...

And ran...

And ran...

Finally, they lost him.

Tommy and Maggie were so tired from running.

They were ready to go home.

They turned the corner and they both saw…

A house, it was their home!

Tommy and Maggie were very happy.

They were safe at last.

Both dogs walked up to the house.

It was time to go to sleep and rest.

Maggie and Tommy went to sleep and dreamed of a new adventure.

LaVergne, TN USA
07 December 2009
166040LV00001B